Mighty Stallion 4
Dancer's Dream

The Sequel to Mighty Stallion 3 – Glory's
Legend

Written By Victoria Kasten

To: Kayla

Love

Victoria J

An exciting new journey begins….

…Dancer, Glory's filly, is ready for her own adventure… Travel west with her as she meets new friends and a special young girl. Will her courage be strong enough when she faces separation from her herd and a frightening storm?

Mighty Stallion 4
Dancer's Dream

The Sequel to Mighty Stallion 3 Glory's Legend

By: Victoria Kasten

Original cover by James Krom Natural Images

First Edition Second Printing • 200 copies • June 2013

Library of Congress
Control Number: 2007902140

ISBN: 978-0-9788850-3-8

Additional copies of this book are available by mail. See back pages for information. Send comments to:

Mighty Stallion Books
1808 Summit Dr NE
Rochester, MN 55906

Published By: Victoria Kasten

Printed in the USA by
Morris Publishing®
3212 East Highway 30
Kearney, NE 68847
1-800-650-7888

Dedicated to
The People of Lonsdale

For your constant support of me and my work…
Thank you!

TABLE OF CONTENTS

1. The Urge

The golden sun's rays beamed over the cave. Songbirds chirped sweetly in the trees, welcoming the start of a new day. A lone white stallion stood under the small waterfall that was in front of the cave's mouth.

Glory stepped out of the water and shook himself, spraying water over the surrounding foliage. Taking a long drink from the pool, he looked up at the blue skies that arched above the forest. So entranced was he by the beautiful scene that he didn't hear the soft hoof beats behind him.

"Dad?" said a quiet voice behind him. Glory flinched, startled out of his daydream by the sound of his daughter's voice. Turning around, he smiled as his yearling daughter, Dancer, stepped out of the cave towards him.

"Hello, Dancer. You're up early," Glory commented. The black filly shook her mane sheepishly.

"I heard you leave the cave. I'm sorry I interrupted you. I know you like to be alone in the morning."

The white stallion snorted. "Don't worry, Dancer. You know that I enjoy your company very much. Are the others awake yet?" he asked, inclining his head towards the cave.

Dancer shook her head again. "No, they are all still asleep. You and I are the only ones up."

Glory sighed as his eyes swept over his daughter. She really was becoming quite lovely. As a very young foal, her coat had been a charcoal gray color, but as she matured, it had darkened to such a dark gray that she was nearly black. Her dark eyes were compassionate and sweet, and her mane and tail were full and very long for her age.

Dancer stepped forward into the pool, letting the water lap comfortingly around her fetlocks.

"Dad, I think…you know the restless feeling you said I would get? The one where I would want to leave and have an adventure? Well…I think I have it now."

Glory felt his heart sink slightly as he looked at his daughter from underneath his long white forelock. But she was so young! She couldn't possibly take care of herself at this age. Glory gently reminded himself that he had been only a little bit older than Dancer when he had left home for the first time. But this was his daughter, his pride and joy…

"Just promise me that you will be very, very careful. Stay out of the way of humans, and don't go anywhere near another herd of horses unless there is no stallion leading them. I don't want my daughter stolen away by a young rogue out west."

Dancer laughed. "Dad, you are such a worrier. I'm not going to go and join another herd! I love it here, and I love all of my friends and my family. Why would I ever want to leave?"

Glory smiled wistfully. "You will understand one day, my dear. Love is a very complicated thing. But I know that someday you will find it. Of that, I am in no doubt."

Dancer looked away, her dark eyes thoughtful. "I don't think I will ever accept a mate. I just want to be free to do as I like."

A deep chuckle came from Glory's throat. "I know, and right now it is natural that you should feel that way. But in the future, I believe that you will see things very differently."

Dancer was about to reply when another horse appeared from the cave entrance. It was Secret, Dancer's mother. The buckskin mare looked from her mate to her daughter curiously.

"You two are up early...what's the occasion?" she asked. Glory smiled at his mate and nuzzled her cheek gently.

"Oh nothing. We're just talking about Dancer's journey. It's about that time now, and she finally discovered the urge to go, so we were just talking about it."

Secret immediately began shaking her head. "Absolutely not. Dancer is not anywhere near old enough to go roaming about the countryside by herself! She could get killed."

Dancer felt hurt by her mother's words. "But Dad had the same urge that I do. He went off on his own at this age. Why can't I?"

Secret lowered her head. "Dancer, darling, you are a filly. Your place is here with your herd. And you are the only daughter I have."

A snort from Glory kept Dancer from replying. "Let's go inside and have breakfast, shall we? We can discuss this more later."

***

Dancer ate her breakfast silently, refusing to converse with any of the other herd members. Secret watched her daughter worriedly throughout the meal. Finally, she saw Dancer move away from the herd and go outside the cave.

The buckskin mare sighed deeply and followed her daughter outside. She found the dark gray filly standing in a little sumac thicket. Secret cleared her throat quietly, and Dancer whirled.

4

"Mom...what are you doing here?" the filly asked sheepishly. Secret didn't answer, but looked up at the leafy canopy above them.

"This thicket brings back a lot of memories from my earlier years. Your father and I used to come here to talk about life. You probably don't remember this, but we brought you here to play sometimes when you were very small."

Dancer frowned. "I remember. Look...I'm sorry that I..." she began to say, but Secret shook her head.

"No, Dancer. Don't be sorry. You can't help wanting to go off and start an adventure of your own. It's a natural part of our lives. I think you should go, providing you take someone with you."

A smile spread over Dancer's face. "You really mean that, don't you?" she asked, as if she were afraid to hope. Secret nodded in affirmation. Dancer squealed and pranced around her mother. Secret couldn't help but smile at the young filly's antics. The older mare turned and walked slowly out of the sumac thicket.

Dancer followed her silently. "Who can I take with me? I don't really have any friends other than the herd, and they are all too old to go."

Secret snorted indignantly. "Too old? I beg your pardon, young filly, but I am barely nine years of age!"

Laughing, the two horses trotted back to the cave entrance.

5

The next morning was the dawn of a new beginning in Dancer's life. As the herd ate their breakfast meal, Glory made an announcement.

"I have decided to visit an old friend of mine, another stallion who lived in my father's herd when we were both young colts. I haven't seen him for almost eight years, and I would like to go. I won't be gone very long, only a few days. I am only taking Dancer and Secret with me."

This caused much murmuring among the horses. Dancer felt excited. She loved to travel, and it would be fun to meet an old friend of her father's. She glanced at Secret, who was standing behind her. The older mare had a twinkle in her eye as she smiled at her daughter. Dancer shrugged it off, but it made her immensely curious. She had seen that look on her mother's face before. It meant something special was going to happen.

Dancer found her father after the meal was over. Walking up to the white stallion, she couldn't help her question of curiosity.

"Dad, how far away is your friend's herd?" she asked. Glory smiled broadly at the question.

"Only a day's journey. Oh, and just so you know…he has a son who is about your age, named Titan."

Dancer gave her sire a meaningful look. "Dad, the fact that your friend has a son my age does not concern me…at all. I am not interested in colts."

With a careless shrug, Glory moved away. Dancer was left feeling very irritated and perplexed. Her parents were acting very strangely. What could be so special about this colt that her parents were that anxious for her to meet him?

Dancer left the main room of the cave, puzzling over it all.

2. Meeting Titan

Dancer was awoken by her sire very early the next morning. Glory blew softly into his daughter's face as she stirred out of her sleep.

"Wake up, princess. It's almost time to go," he whispered in her ear. She sighed wearily as she lurched to her feet. Shaking herself, she tried to force her eyes to focus, for they were very blurry still because of her drowsiness.

"I'm coming. Will we reach your friend's herd by dark?" the dark gray filly wanted to know. Glory looked uncertain.

"I'm not sure, Dancer. I think we might, but you never know what sort of obstacles we might meet on the way. It could very well take us a couple of days, if your mother and I decide to take a couple of detours along the way."

Dancer groaned involuntarily, causing her sire to laugh heartily. Glory left the room, still chuckling. Dancer shook her head and followed him out to the cave's mouth, where the herd was waiting to say goodbye.

Fury stood at the head of the group of horses, and Dancer immediately noted the twinkle in her grandsire's eye. She smiled at him warmly, and he returned the gesture. Turning to Glory, the old red stallion began to speak.

"We will look for your return after the completion of many days. Stay with your friends as long as you wish. We will look after things here while you are gone," he said. Then he turned to Dancer.

"Listen to your parents. The world is a very dangerous place, and they have been in it longer than you. They are wise, and can protect you, even if you do not believe it. And above all, have a wonderful time on your journey. I'm sure you'll make a lot of new friends," Fury finished, winking at his grandfilly.

Dancer humphed. Was her family ever going to stop acting so silly? She had no interest in a mate. She saw a warning look on Secret's face, and apologized to her grandsire.

"Thank you for your wise words, Grandfather. I will remember them. And I'm sure I'll make a lot of new *friends* too," she replied, putting a heavy emphasis on the

10

second to last word. This brought chuckles of amusement from the herd members, who caught on to the joke.

Glory and Secret began trotting west, and Dancer dutifully followed them, keeping a little ways behind. She heard the farewell neighing of the herd from behind her, and smiled to herself. She was going to miss her friends and family from the cave, but she was sure that she would have fun on this little adventure with her parents.

***

The first day of travel was uneventful for the three horses. Just as the last golden sun's rays were fading from view behind the mountains, Glory stopped the two mares in a small grove of evergreen trees. Dancer wearily sank to the ground, her legs aching from all the unaccustomed exercise.

"How much farther?" she asked quietly. Secret, who had also settled down to rest on the forest floor, smiled at her daughter's question.

"Ever the impatient one. We'll get there when we get there, Dancer. So don't worry yourself about it."

Glory shook his head in amusement. "Don't rebuke her, Secret. She's just excited to see a new place and new horses. There will be a lot of excitement once we get there, and she knows that. Right, Dancer?" he asked the filly.

But it was too late. Dancer was fast asleep; exhausted from all the traveling they'd done that day. Glory smiled and looked at Secret, who gave him a very meaningful stare.

"We should be doing the same thing," she said. Glory chuckled and lay down on the ground next to his mate, caressing her neck with his muzzle.

"Of course, my beauty."

Secret smiled. "We have another full day of travel tomorrow if we are supposed to get there while the day's still young. Dancer didn't notice that we took the long way around the prairie so we could enjoy the scenery a little longer."

Glory sighed. "No, and that's a good thing, too. We would've never heard the end of it!"

Stifling their mirth, the two older horses slowly dropped off into a deep slumber.

***

It was not long after the sun had risen over the treetops that the three horses were again on their way towards the wide valley where Glory's colthood friend lived. As they walked, Dancer decided to find out more about this horse and his family.

12

"So, Father, what is your friend's name?" she asked curiously. Glory looked over his shoulder at her and smiled.

"His name is Fleetstar. He and I used to race each other around the meadow when we were colts. He always beat me, because he was older and faster than I was. When I was finally old enough to challenge him properly, he got the urge to go on his journey, and never returned. It was only recently that one of the horses from our herd told me that Fleetstar was living with his own herd only a day's journey away from our own."

Dancer pondered this for a moment, falling silent.

Glory continued, "I think you'll like Fleetstar's son. His name is Titan. I hear he's a very good looking colt."

Dancer's head came up sharply. "I don't understand why you are so anxious for me to meet Fleetstar's son."

There was no comment from her parents, and Dancer shook her head in exasperation. And suddenly, she realized why they had been talking about it so much. She spoke again, her tone slightly angry.

"I'm not going to choose him as a mate, you know. I have absolutely no interest in any stallion at all. So please don't say anything more about it."

If Glory or Secret had planned on answering, their words faded as the three horses stopped at the top of a high ridge and looked down over a deep, sloping valley below. Dancer gasped at the beautiful sight. At the far end of the valley, they could see a huge forest. Nearer to Dancer and her parents was a wide prairie-like meadow.

In this meadow was a very large herd of horses, bigger than any Dancer had ever seen.

Dancer saw all different ages, sizes, and colors of horses in the meadow. There were many chestnuts, bays, grays, paints, palominos, and buckskins. Dancer was surprised to notice that there were no blacks among them, but didn't have time to think about it, because Glory and Secret went lunging down the steep trail that led to the valley floor.

Dancer hurriedly raced after them, being extra careful not to slip and fall, for it was quite a long ways down.

Reaching the meadow, Glory and Secret stopped, for now the herd had seen them, and there were whinnies of welcome from all around the three newcomers. A big gray stallion approached them, a look of surprise and delight on his handsome features.

"Glory, is that you? Worlds of wonder, but you've grown a sight since our last meeting! And whom have you brought with you? Ahhh, don't tell me. This is your daughter. I can see the resemblance very clearly," he said.

Glory laughed. "Greetings to you too, old friend. I should very well hope that I've grown; since the last time you saw me I was barely a yearling! This is my mate, Secret, and you've already identified my daughter. Her name is Dancer."

Fleetstar's eyes twinkled as they grazed swiftly over the filly. Dancer felt slightly uneasy under the stallion's gaze, but she stood tall and proud.

"It is indeed a pleasure to make your acquaintance, sir. My father has informed me that you were his playmate in colthood."

Fleetstar smiled. "Dancer, you are very gifted in the use of words. Such maturity for a filly your age is quite uncommon. It is very wonderful to meet you. I always knew that any offspring of Glory's would be very impressive. It's hardly surprising, considering your ancestry."

Dancer felt very proud at the stallion's assessment of her. She had always felt so privileged to carry the bloodline of the great mustang stallion Sariavo. Now, she felt almost famous, because her ancestry was known far and wide by almost every horse herd in the west.

Fleetstar began introducing Glory and Secret to the members of his herd, but Dancer was too busy looking up at the high valley walls and the forest, which was almost a mile away.

Three forms emerged from the treeline, racing for the herd as fast as they could run. Dancer strained her eyes to make out exactly what the figures were. She gasped aloud as she realized that they were horses. But the speed at which they were traveling was nearly supernatural.

Dancer watched, spellbound, as the three horses came closer and closer, and became more and more visible. She saw that the horse in the lead was midnight black, a brilliant shade of ebony that she had never seen before. The horse held her gaze; she couldn't look away from the awesome sight.

15

The three horses thundered into the midst of the herd and slid to a stop, blowing and breathing hard. Dancer quickly averted her eyes as the big black colt looked directly at her.

Fleetstar stepped forward. "Titan, what did you find? Anything of interest?"

The big colt lowered his head respectfully. "Many wagons are passing by on the other side of the valley, Father. They all are going west, with many, many people. In this group there were almost fifty humans."

The gray stallion sighed deeply as he considered this. The whole herd was silent, watching their leader. Dancer glanced at Titan, and caught the colt staring at her. She gave him an irritated look, and he quickly looked away. Fleetstar saw this, and Dancer felt as small as an ant when she saw the disappointment that clouded his eyes. The filly immediately felt guilty for being so negative towards Titan.

Fleetstar's voice broke through the stillness. "The humans move farther and farther west every year. Very soon, there will be nowhere left for the wild horses to live."

The herd murmured sadly at this. The statement was not a surprise to any of the horses. They had known that their freedom was in jeopardy for many years.

Dancer felt tears well up in her eyes. She couldn't imagine life without her freedom. Her parents had always taught her that freedom was not a state of being, but a state of mind. No matter who enslaved her physically, no human could ever take away the freedom of her heart.

Dancer's thoughts were interrupted by Fleetstar's next announcement. "We will move up into the forested hills for safety. I will not see any of my herd captured by the humans. We all remember Lily, who was taken by a wagon train guide."

A hush fell over the herd at the name. Dancer felt very confused. She looked at her sire questioningly.

"Father, who is Lily?" she asked curiously. Glory didn't get a chance to answer, for Titan spoke up.

"Father, that is the other news that I have brought for you," the colt said, his voice full of hesitation. Fleetstar looked up at his son.

"What is the news, my son?"

Titan continued. "Lily is with them. She is tied to one of the wagons that are in the group passing by us right now."

Fleetstar gasped in shock. "My daughter? Here? Then we will not let her be taken any farther. Titan, gather every able-bodied herd member together, and ready them. We are going to free her! The old and the very young will stay behind and go up into the hills. We will join them after we have liberated Lily from the wagon train."

Titan's eyes glowed with the prospect of battle. He immediately began obeying his father's order, sorting the herd members into two groups, one to free Lily, and the other to go up into the hills and wait for the combatants to return.

When Titan came to Glory, Secret, and Dancer, he looked uncertain. Glory smiled and spoke.

"I will help you rescue your sister, Titan."

Secret nodded mutely. Dancer stepped forward, and looked the big black colt square in the eye.

"As will I."

Titan looked at her in surprise, and then his expression turned doubtful. Secret was very strong in her own opinions of the matter.

"Absolutely not! You will not go with them! You are a two-year-old filly, Dancer. Your place is with me and the others that are going up into the hills. Do you understand me?" she said vehemently. Dancer's eyes narrowed.

"Father?" she said quietly, knowing that he held the final say. Glory looked from one mare to the other, unsure of what to do. Dancer stood as tall as she good, and tried to look fierce. Glory sighed.

"Very well. You may come with us. After all, you are a great granddaughter of Sariavo. You are a warhorse by blood."

Secret opened her mouth to protest, but Glory whispered something quickly in her ear. The buckskin mare shook her head, and left to join the other herd members who were beginning to make the journey into the forests. Dancer felt euphoria bubbling up inside her. She was going with her father! She was going to help free Lily!

3. Lily

The wagon train rumbled along noisily. Shouts from the wagon drivers, a baby crying, the creaking of the wheels and the grunts of the mules that pulled the heavy loads made for a horrible din.

The well-concealed wild horses watched all this from their hiding places next to the trail. The thick foliage rendered them invisible to the wagons. Dancer found herself standing between her sire and Titan. She kept her eyes focused on the wagons, but she couldn't help glancing at the black colt several times. She still didn't know what to think of him.

Her thoughts were interrupted by Glory's whisper. "Dancer, when we move in, you stay with me, and don't go running off by yourself. You stay right beside me, do you understand?" he said, his tone giving no room for argument. Dancer nodded silently.

Fleetstar stood a little ways off, waiting for Lily to appear so he could give the signal to attack.

Finally, the chestnut filly came into view, tied behind a wagon pulled by two mules. Lily had a tightly bound rope halter tied around her slim face, and she docilely followed the wagon, all the fight gone from her eyes.

Dancer felt fury rising within her. How dare the humans treat a horse this way! The black filly's anger was not unnoticed by Titan, who stared at her in surprise as her eyes narrowed.

The cracks of whips kept the weary mules going; slowly but surely the train of wagons scraped along the rock hard ground. Fleetstar saw his daughter, and his eyes darkened. Lifting his muzzle high in the air, he bellowed. The sound echoed through the trees and sent the humans into a panic.

Instantly, the entire wagon trail was in an uproar. All the wild horses lunged out of the forest, ears flat back against their heads, teeth bared, eyes rolled white. The main group distracted the humans while a group of four horses fought towards Lily, who had now recognized the herd and was trying to free herself. These four horses were Dancer, Glory, Titan and Fleetstar. The stallions were blocked by three wagon guides, who leveled their guns at the horses.

Without even a second thought, Dancer plowed through the gunmen and raced towards Lily. She reared up and brought her hooves down on the board to which Lily's halter was tied, smashing the wood to bits.

Dancer grabbed the loose lead rope in her teeth and pulled Lily along with her, back towards the forest. The herd, seeing that the fillies were clear of the wagon train, retreated speedily into the trees.

Quiet slowly descended back down on the wagons. The humans stared in disbelief towards the woods where the horses had disappeared. After quickly checking over the train's occupants, the guides hurriedly got the wagons moving again.

Back behind the shelter of the trees, her herd surrounded Lily, all asking her questions and expressing their relief at her return.

Fleetstar pushed through the crowded horses and found his daughter. Blinking back tears of joy, the gray stallion gently nuzzled Lily's cheek. Tears rolled down the chestnut filly's face, falling like tiny raindrops to the forest floor.

"Welcome home, daughter," Fleetstar said lovingly. Lily nodded mutely, obviously fighting to keep her composure. Titan appeared at her left side and smiled at her.

"Hello, little sister. How many times have I told you not to go wandering off alone?" he teased her, his eyes sparkling. Lily's eyes brightened.

"Titan!" she exclaimed happily, overjoyed to see her brother. But then, Lily's eyes searched the horses gathered before her for someone else. The herd moved back, pushing Dancer forward. The black filly ducked her head down, embarrassed at the attention. Lily looked at Dancer, her eyes filled with inexpressible gratitude.

"Thank you for saving me. I owe you my freedom," Lily said quietly. Dancer brought her head up slightly, feeling very uncomfortable.

"Please, don't mention it. I did nothing that any other horse in this herd would not have done. Any one of them could've saved you, not just me."

Lily shook her red mane stubbornly. "But it was you. Please, tell me your name?" she asked.

"I'm Dancer, daughter of Glory. We're from the herd of Sariavo."

Fleetstar rescued Dancer from any further embarrassment by interrupting the conversation.

"Well, there will be plenty of time for introductions later. But now, I think we should all join up with the rest of the herd. They'll be up in the hills by now, and I do believe that there will be a very big celebration when Lily is reunited with the rest of our family. Glory, Dancer, you two must accompany us. And Dancer will be our guest of honor for the remainder of your stay, as my thanks for her bravery."

***

Fleetstar did not forget his promise. When the herd was reunited, everyone treated Dancer with respect and gratitude. The young filly didn't necessarily approve of the situation, but she decided it wasn't so bad being pampered. Lily was received back into her family with much joy, and there was a celebration among the horses that night.

Secret found Dancer and smiled warmly. "It would seem that I was wrong to misjudge you, my dear. Fleetstar has told me of your bravery, and how you saved Lily," she said. Dancer felt the heat rise in her face.

"He over exaggerates my part. I wasn't that brave. The other horses did most of the work. I just happened to be in the right place at the right time. Nothing more."

Secret smiled again, shaking her ebony mane. "Perhaps. I must say, however, you certainly impressed one of the herd members," she said, her eyes shifting to the other side of the clearing, where Titan stood beside his sister. The black colt was watching Dancer intently, his dark eyes studying her.

The filly tossed her mane and looked away. Secret sighed. "You know, Dancer, he's a very nice colt…" her voice trailed off as she saw Dancer hang her head sadly.

"Mother please…I'm sure he'll make a fine mate for a filly someday. But it won't be me."

Dancer said no more, and moved away to join another group of horses. Secret shook her head in exasperation.

***

Titan approached Dancer. She looked up at him suspiciously.

"Can I help you?" she asked, her tone bordering on unfriendly. Titan looked slightly surprised at her hostile manner, and seemed to rethink his words. His eyes seemed to question her, and that bothered Dancer.

"Do you have something to say?" she asked. Titan sighed and nodded.

"Your parents mentioned that you would like to go on a journey soon. They also said that they would feel much more at ease should you travel with a companion. I was just wondering if Lily and I could come along and be your companions."

Dancer was taken aback by the request. She didn't know what to say. If she allowed Titan and Lily to join her, no doubt her parents would see that as a sign of her liking for Titan. But she realized that she needed them if she hoped to go on her journey.

"I suppose it would be fine."

Titan smiled warmly, sending an unexpected shiver through Dancer's spine. She shook herself to clear it away. Titan walked away to tell Lily that they were going. Dancer watched him go curiously. Why had he volunteered to come with her? She shook her head in bewilderment.

***

It didn't take long for Titan, Dancer and Lily to say their goodbyes to the herd and start on their way. Secret and Glory had given their daughter many pieces of advice before her departure. Dancer's head was so full of things to remember that she could hardly think straight. Fleetstar had been reluctant to part with Lily now that she was finally back with the herd. Lily had assured him that she would be very careful and always stay with Dancer and Titan, and this seemed to ease Fleetstar's worry somewhat.

The three companions set off into the forests silently. No words were spoken by any of them, and the air held a slight quaver of tension. Dancer did not look at Titan, and tried to keep up a steady pace as they traveled. The day passed with few delays and no obstacles. Dancer wasn't really sure where they were going; all she knew was that she wanted to go somewhere.

Titan and Lily followed her without question, only inquiring about the general direction of their journey.

For two days, it was very quiet among the three horses, and not much was said. But on the third day, something happened that made them all come closer together.

Dancer was trotting a little ways ahead of Lily and Titan, scouting out their path of travel, when she noticed that the forest had grown suddenly quiet. Not even a bird chirped in the trees. Everything was still except for one sound. To Dancer's left in the bushes, there was a grunting and snuffling sound. The filly's blood ran cold as a low growl emitted from the undergrowth.

A brown snout appeared from behind a pine tree, followed by the brown shaggy body of a bear.

The huge grizzly was an adult male, looking for an easy kill. He saw Dancer and his beady black eyes glowed savagely. The filly moved very slowly, taking one tiny backward step at a time. She knew that if she ran, the bear would lunge for her, and she was too close to get away in time.

Titan and Lily appeared through the trees, unaware of the danger. Dancer was panicked. She couldn't alert them to the bear's presence without jeopardizing her own safety. But they were her friends. Dancer's blood ran hot with the anticipation of battle that had been coursing through her ancestors since far before Sariavo.

Without a second thought, she charged just as the bear lunged forward.

4. A Deed of Valor

Dancer felt cold. Her eyes fluttered open and she tried to focus on the bleary shapes that wafted before her vision. Vaguely she recalled the bear, and she struggled slightly, and was immediately pressed back down by a hard object that she recognized as a hoof.

"Dancer, if you can hear me, don't struggle."

The filly immediately ceased her movements and lay still. Her eyes became a little bit more focused, and she saw that Titan was standing over her, his dark eyes filled with worry. Lily stood beside him.

"What..." Dancer managed to ask. Titan quickly responded.

"You attacked the grizzly. I don't know how you did it, but you managed to hit him with your hooves. He tore your shoulder open. It's a deep wound, but it will heal with time."

Dancer sighed deeply, and her eyes closed again, welcoming the peaceful depths of sleep.

∗∗∗

Over the next few days, Dancer was almost totally immobile. Titan wouldn't let her do anything except go to the little spring of water for a drink, which was a very slow and painful process for the filly. Her shoulder now bore tough scabs that covered the hidden wounds beneath.

Slowly but surely, the gashes healed, leaving long pink scars in their place. Dancer would walk with a slight limp for the rest of her life, but as Lily pointed out, she was fortunate just to be alive. Dancer began to exercise her stiff limbs now that her shoulder was mostly healed, trying to regain her strength and balance.

Titan supervised her closely, making sure that she didn't overdo things. Lily kept herself busy by helping Dancer along, telling jokes to make the other filly laugh.

After four weeks of healing, the time eventually came when Dancer felt well enough to continue the journey. The three horses started off, leaving the little oak grove that had become home to them for the time that they had been helping Dancer recover.

The forest ended abruptly and became a wide, rolling prairie. Tall grass rose to the horses' knees, brushing lightly against their forelegs. Everything seemed so open and spacious compared to the forest. Titan galloped through the grass, parting it with his strong black legs. A few hundred yards from the two fillies, he stopped. He buckled his knees and eased himself down to the warm grasses, and began rolling.

Dancer laughed and did the same, snorting with pleasure as the grass soothed away her stiffness and itches. Lily chuckled at the two of them.

"You two look so silly. Besides, how are you going to get up now?" she asked teasingly. Dancer easily rolled to one side and lurched to her feet stiffly. She grunted with the effort. Though her shoulder had healed, it was still hard for her to move in certain ways. Lily gave her a worried look, but said nothing. Dancer watched as Titan stood up, and shook himself heartily, ridding his ebony coat of the dust and dirt.

Lily giggled slightly, and kicked up her heels. Dancer smiled and snaked her head down playfully. Lily took up the challenge, and the two fillies took off, running free, their manes streaming back behind them, their light hooves skimming over the prairie, not even seeming to touch the earth.

Dancer drew ahead slightly, and Lily struggled to keep up. Finally, the dark gray filly decided to see how fast she could run. Her dark legs went faster, her ears swept back against her head; the wind whipped her mane back. Lily dropped far behind in the wake of the darker filly, who seemed to be flying.

When Dancer finally slowed, she looked over her shoulder to see Titan and Lily galloping towards her, amazement showing on their faces. When Dancer's two companions reached her, Lily spoke first.

"Dancer, you were so fast! I've never seen any horse run like that in my whole life! Not even my father could've beaten you!" she exclaimed in wonder. Titan seconded his sister's opinion.

"I agree with Lily, Dancer. You have a rare gift. You were flying!" he said with a smile. Dancer looked at the two of them excitedly. Flying? She had sure felt like it. The three horses continued on their way, talking like they had been friends for years. Dancer felt the tension of the earlier days vanish as she kept up an easy conversation with her two companions.

***

Midday came and passed, leaving the hot afternoon sun to beam unmercifully down on the travelers. Soon, all three horses were sweating heavily, the scorching rays draining strength from their bodies.

Lily was practically dragging herself along behind her brother. Titan had slowed their pace quite a bit, and Dancer was thankful. Occasionally, Titan would glance back at the two fillies to make sure they were still keeping up.

When the borderline of the next forest was in sight, all three horses gave a short whinny of joy, and rushed forward, drawing upon the last reserves of their strength. They reached the trees just as the night began to fall, and found a small spring of water. Drinking thirstily, they surveyed their surroundings curiously.

The forest was not much different from the one that they had just left. Birds sang cheerfully from the treetops, and the chattering of squirrels sounded from above the three horses. The water was clear and cool, a welcome refreshment to the weary travelers.

"I think we should sleep here tonight," said Titan quietly to the two fillies. They nodded wearily and sank to the ground. Titan followed suit, but kept his eyes alert to the forest around them. He had no interest in repeating the episode with the bear.

But soon, sleep overtook him, and he fell into a deep slumber.

***

Morning came, bringing with it the warmth of the sun, which was welcome to the travelers in the forest. Dancer rose and stretched out her neck, releasing the stiffness from it. She shook herself, and took a drink from the stream. Titan was the next to wake, and he smiled at Dancer.

31

"Good morning," he said cordially. Dancer smiled back, and then looked away, feeling the heat rise in her face. She was beginning to think of Titan as a friend... maybe more. Shaking her head, she was surprised at herself. Only weeks ago she had vowed never to find a mate, but Titan was so kind and thoughtful.

Lily suddenly awoke with a huge yawn, exposing her teeth. She lurched up, and drowsily drank from the spring, still not fully awake. She stumbled around a bit until she finally began to snap out of her trance. Titan shook his head at his sister.

"She always was a heavy sleeper. She could've slept through a forest fire and never heard a thing," he teased her good-naturedly. Lily glared at him.

"I would too. You're just being annoying," she told him matter-of-factly. Dancer laughed at the pair of them. They were so funny together, and always teased each other without mercy. But then, Dancer guessed, that was what brothers and sisters did. She found herself wishing that she had had a brother or sister to play with and tease.

"Dancer, are you ready to leave?" Lily asked, noticing that her friend seemed to be deep in thought. The dark filly looked up and nodded.

"Yes, I'm ready to go. Where are we going now?" she asked Titan, who shook his mane.

"It's your journey, Dancer. You lead the way." His eyes sparkled at her, and Dancer quickly began walking, trying to escape the awkward feeling that was bubbling up inside her. She was not going to look like a fool in

32

front of Titan. What a notion…Titan didn't love her. Of that she was certain.

Ridding her mind of such thoughts, Dancer focused on the trail ahead. A distant rumble reached her ears. She recognized it instantly. It was the sound of wagons as they passed along the trails. Her ears swept back and she looked over her shoulder at Lily and Titan. Lily knew the sound as well, and her eyes widened slightly in fright. Titan nickered reassuringly at her, and then looked up at Dancer. The dark filly sighed and lowered herself to the forest floor.

"We will rest here until the wagons pass."

***

The night was cool and quiet, but Dancer could not sleep. She tried hard to close her eyes, but something kept her awake. Finally, she stood and began walking into the trees. She didn't notice that she was being followed.

She wandered among the trees, her hooves barely making a sound on the forest floor. The wind rustled the leaves slightly as it blew among the treetops. A twig snapped, and Dancer whirled around.

A dark shape loomed up before her in the brush. With a snort of terror, Dancer turned to run…

"Might I inquire as to why you are wandering about the forest alone?" asked a familiar voice. Dancer instantly relaxed; it was Titan. The black stallion stepped forward into the moonlight. The shaft of light illuminated his ebony coat, making him glow a shiny blue-black color. Dancer barely kept from openly staring at the magnificent sight.

Dancer quickly composed herself and looked down at her hooves. "I couldn't sleep," she admitted, somewhat guiltily. Titan's eyes softened and he nodded.

"I didn't want you to get lost," he said. An uncomfortable silence followed his words, before Titan spoke again. "Dancer...I know that you might think me just a friend, but I had hoped...perhaps..." his voice trailed off into silence. Dancer stared at him in disbelief.

"You had hoped what?" she asked quietly, stepping a bit closer to the stallion. Titan looked at her questioningly.

"I had hoped that perhaps we could be even closer than friends," he said softly, looking into Dancer's dark eyes. The filly caught her breath, her eyes widening slightly in amazement. She had never expected anything like this. She now realized how important Titan had become to her.

"Are you asking me something?" she questioned teasingly, trying desperately to keep her voice light. Titan smiled warmly at her and nodded. Dancer lowered her eyes. The stallion finally spoke the words that they both had been waiting to hear.

"Would you consider me as your mate?"

***

Lily was overjoyed when they told her the news. Her reaction had been the true completion of Dancer's own happiness. But she knew that the horses that would welcome the news most would be her parents. They had hoped for such a match for a long time.

Titan seemed to radiate excitement as they hurried back towards their home. They had been on the journey for long enough in Dancer's opinion, and now she wanted nothing more than to see her family again. Titan and Lily were in whole-hearted agreement.

They traveled swiftly, reaching the prairie at night and traveling through it during the dark hours to avoid the scorching sun. They crossed it with little difficulty, but were not aware of the stalkers that followed them.

It was not until they had almost reached the edge of the second forest that they were aware of the sudden danger. The three horses had stopped to rest for a few minutes, when four humans on horseback came galloping over the hill in front of them, whirling their lassoes.

Titan and Lily lunged into a run, racing away. Dancer tried to follow, but she tripped over a stone and fell heavily to her side. Looking over his shoulder, Titan saw this, and whirled around. Lily screamed at her brother to stop, but the stallion kept going. As he neared the men who were throwing ropes around Dancer's neck, he bared his teeth and snaked his head forward menacingly. The men shouted and tossed several ropes, which fell neatly over the stallion's head and secured him easily.

Titan's rage at being captured was insatiable. He bellowed in anger and reared, striking out with heavy forefeet at the nearest man. The cowboy laughed heartily and backed up his mount, keeping easily out of the stallion's range.

Dancer looked up sadly at the struggling stallion. Her despair was evident, for she knew that had it not been for her, Titan would have gone free. She could not rise, for two cowboys had thrown a rope about one of her legs, and should she try to get up, they would simply pull the rope and make her fall.

"Titan," she whispered. The stallion heard her voice and stopped fighting the cowboys. He looked down at her, and the fire in his eyes dimmed slightly. The men could not understand the horse's language; to them Dancer's softly spoken word sounded like a quiet nicker.

Instead, they began laughing heartily. "Lookit 'ere, boys! One little sound from thet mare and 'e goes all quiet like!" one of them shouted mockingly. "She must be 'is sweetheart!"

Titan's ears swept back again warningly as he charged toward one of his captors ferociously. The men stopped laughing as a fifth cowboy rode into their midst, obviously the leader.

"Alright boys, time to head back to the camp. We've got a lot of work to do if we're going to break these mustangs by the end of the week," he said smoothly. Dancer noted that he didn't talk like the other cowboys. His speech was considerably cleaner and not so rough.

She glared at him as he passed her. The cowboy looked down at her where she lay captive on the ground and grinned slightly.

"I'll break the mare," he said, and turned his gelding around, trotting off over the hill. Titan bellowed again as the cowboys began pulling the two horses after their boss. Dancer's hoof was released from its rope, and she was roughly hauled along after two cowboys, her ropes attached to their saddle horns.

Dancer knew that Lily was safe, and that gave her some amount of happiness. But as for the fate of Titan and herself…it was a bleak prospect.

5. Break The Mare

Dancer and Titan were led all the way to a wagon camp a few miles away from the place of their captivity. Through the talk between the men that had captured them, the horses learned that the cowboys were guides for the wagon train that they were being taken to as packhorses and mounts.

The cowboys finally led them into the clearing that was the temporary home of the wagons. Many people were gathered around a fire, several women were cooking a delicious smelling stew in a large cauldron over the flames. Children ran around amongst the wagons, laughing.

Dancer stared at the sight before her. She had never seen so many humans all together at once. She glanced at

Titan, who gave her a helpless look. Dancer knew that she and Titan had very little chance of escaping.

One of the girls from the wagon train came up and looked at the new horses wonderingly. She stayed a respectful distance, obviously aware of the mustangs' unpredictability. The girl was about fourteen, and she had lopsided brown braids and bright green eyes. Dancer felt drawn to this girl somehow. Why, she didn't know. The mustang mare reached out her nose gently towards the girl. Before anyone could stop her, the girl extended her hand and touched the mare's nose.

Dancer's eyes gently surveyed the girl, and she blew out a soft breath into the girl's face. The girl giggled and then turned and ran back to one of the wagons. The cowboys were speechless.

Then the moment passed and Dancer became the wild horse again. She pulled against her ropes violently, still hoping to perhaps have a chance at breaking free. But the cowboys tied her tightly to a post just outside the camp. Titan was similarly bound, a rope halter about his head.

The two horses were left alone as the cowboys made their way to the fire to get their supper.

Dancer strained against her ropes, and found that they were long enough that she could reach Titan comfortably. He moved closer to her, and the two horses gently touched their foreheads together.

"I'm so sorry, Titan," Dancer whispered despairingly. She knew that if it hadn't been for her, Titan would be free. But the stallion merely smiled slightly. "Don't be. I should've known better than to let down my guard when we were so close to a wagon train. It's as much my fault as yours. At least Lily is safe, and we are together. It could've been much worse," he said, trying to lift her spirits.

Dancer nodded silently. Titan felt worried about her. "Dancer, I promise you, we will escape from this place. I promise…" he said softly, his eyes gazing into hers.

A soft step sounded from a nearby wagon. The horses started, and then realized that it was the young girl who had touched Dancer earlier. The girl sat down about ten feet from the horses, and looked at them curiously. Her eyes flickered over Dancer, and a smile came to her lips.

"You sure are a beautiful horse," said the girl. Dancer felt complimented and nickered quietly. The girl smiled again.

"I wish I could ride you. I had a horse once, back in Missouri. But we couldn't bring him along with us, so Papa gave him to my cousins. I hope they're treating him well. Sometimes my boy cousins can be terrible pests."

Dancer felt calmed by the rich, smooth tone of the girl's voice. Titan was similarly comforted. The girl stood up and walked forward, raising her hand slowly. Dancer shoved her muzzle into the girl's palm. The girl giggled and patted Dancer's neck softly.

41

"I'm Rosie. I think I'll call you Lady, because you're so pretty," said the girl. Dancer snorted quietly, her eyelids beginning to droop as sleep overtook her. She didn't even feel the goodnight pat that Rosie gave her before going back to her wagon.

***

The days that followed were bleak for Titan and Dancer. The wagons continued moving farther west. Dancer did not struggle any more, since she knew that it was pointless.

After a long while, they reached a fort. There were many trappers there, as well as several families. The horses were objects of grave interest. The people all stared at them. Titan and Dancer both felt very uncomfortable.

The man that was the leader of the cowboys took Dancer's rope and led her to a corral. Letting her go inside the corral, he took off her ropes. Dancer felt suspicious. Why was he setting her free? Then she realized what he meant to do as he set a bridle and saddle on the fence. She bared her teeth and whipped her ears back, looking very menacing. The onlookers guffawed.

"She knows what's comin', Bill!" they shouted with laughter. The cowboy smiled smugly at Dancer as though he was facing the task with great anticipation. He tossed one rope around Dancer's neck and held onto it tightly. Using one hand, he managed to get the bridle looped around her head and shoved the bit into her mouth.

Dancer fought wildly, her eyes rolling white with scare. She screamed and tried to rear. Titan was proving to be a difficulty as well, for he fought his captors, trying to get to his mate. The cowboys were having a hard time controlling him, and enlisted the help of several strong traders to hold him.

Dancer flung her head sideways, trying to rid herself of the cold metal bit in her mouth. She kicked out, making the fence rails shake violently. Bill tied the rope to a post and grabbed the saddle. He threw the leather up onto the mare's back, and grabbed the cinch. He ducked, barely missing Dancer's flying hind leg. He jerked the cinch up and stepped back, letting go of the rope and untying it from the post.

He jumped over the fence rails and out of the corral just as Dancer's teeth snapped an inch from his face. He stepped back, breathing heavily, and smiled.

"You see, even the wildest horse can be controlled. It just takes time and patience," he said. Dancer retreated to the far corner of the corral. The cinch had been drawn up so tightly that she could hardly breathe. Blood trickled from the corner of her mouth where the bit rings had chaffed.

The small crowd dispersed, leaving the mare alone. Titan was tied in the corral next to her. The black stallion lunged against the fence, trying to break through, but the wood was sturdy and did not give way. Titan leaned against the rails.

"Dancer!" he whinnied helplessly, furious that he could not reach her. The mare was now feeling the effects of the much too tight girth, and her eyes lifted very slowly as she struggled to breathe. She could not answer him, but her eyes met his and she gave him a reassuring look.

***

Night fell, and with it brought new struggles for the two horses. They had not been fed, and Dancer's breathing was now shallow and pained. Titan stayed as close to her as he could get, but still could do nothing. The fence rails were too tall for him to jump over, and he could not break through them.

Around midnight, a dark shadow moved toward Dancer's corral. The mare raised tortured eyes to see what it was. As the figure moved out of the darkness, Dancer saw that it was Rosie. The girl raised one hand.

"Easy, girl. I'm going to loosen that cinch for you. Just a minute," she said, climbing carefully inside the rails. Dancer stood perfectly still as the girl's fingers fumbled with the buckles.

Finally, the saddle cinch loosened considerably, and Dancer sucked in huge gulps of air. She knew one thing

44

for sure: she would never take such a simple pleasure for granted ever again. Rosie knelt down and gravely inspected the deep cuts in Dancer's side from the cinch. Anger glowed from the girl's green eyes.

"How could he?" she whispered in disbelief. "What a horrid man! I told Papa that he was not a kind man when we started this journey. How could he do this to such a beautiful horse?"

Dancer softly lipped the girl's brown braid. Rosie patted the mare's sleek neck reassuringly.

"Don't you worry, Lady. I'll make sure that you are treated much better. Here, I brought you something," she said, producing a carrot from her pocket. Dancer took the treat appreciatively, her teeth crunching down on the tasty morsel. The mare saw Titan in the other corral, watching all that went on with great interest. Dancer whickered at him, and he answered quietly. Rosie smiled.

"Is that your mate?" she asked. Dancer bobbed her head up and down. Rosie gasped in surprise.

"You know what I said, don't you?" she asked in amazement. Dancer nodded again. Rosie laughed softly in excitement. Without another word, she turned and climbed over the fence rails and ran back towards her parents' wagon. The mare watched her go sadly. She wished that Rosie would not have left so soon, but she knew that the girl didn't want to get caught.

Dancer leaned over her fence rails, and Titan did the same. Their muzzles were only a foot or two apart. Titan sighed deeply.

45

"We're always so close, but never quite there." His voice was edged with despair. Dancer looked worriedly at him, not quite understanding his words. She leaned back slightly.

"What do you mean?"

"We were nearly to the herd when we were captured, we nearly escaped, and now we are nearly able to be close to each other, but we're never quite there. I don't know. It just gets frustrating after a while."

Dancer nodded. "I know what you mean. But I know that we will eventually get our old life back. I'm sure of it. It may take time, but if we believe that it can happen, it will."

Titan smiled at her. "I hope you're right. But for now, I think we should get some sleep. If tomorrow is anything like today, we're going to need all the strength we can get."

The gray mare backed up into the center of her corral. She whole-heartedly agreed with her mate on the fact that sleep was a very welcome prospect. The two horses lay down, and were soon fast asleep.

***

"Get the mare up!"

The voice was harsh and grating to Dancer's ears as she awoke from her slumber. Her eyes shifted from side to side as she took in the scene before her. The cowboys were lounging on the fence rail as they watched Bill move towards her, rope in hand.

Dancer struggled to her feet, stiff from sleeping all night with the saddle strapped to her back. She flattened her ears warningly at the cowboy, who kept advancing toward her. Dancer bared her teeth. Bill ignored the gesture and grabbed the reins of the bridle in his hand. Dancer swung her head around to bite him, but the seasoned cowboy simply smacked her neck.

Before the mare knew what was happening, Bill had his foot in the stirrup and hoisted himself into the saddle. Then came the explosion.

Furious at the cowboy's victory, Dancer reared up, and then took off around the corral, bucking, lunging, kicking and jumping. Bill managed to stay on without too much difficulty until Dancer got down to roll. He leaped free, and then remounted as she rolled back to her feet.

The mare went around the corral again. The cowboys at the fence leaped back as the dust flew up from beneath Dancer's hooves. Rosie sat beside her wagon and watched the proceedings, tears streaming from her eyes.

Suddenly the girl jumped up and ran for the fence rails. She climbed up over them and into the corral, ignoring the frantic shouts of her parents and the cowboys as they tried to grab her. Rosie stopped in the middle of the corral, and Dancer saw her. The mare slid to a stop, trembling, her entire body shaking with exhaustion. Rosie looked up at Bill, her face contorted with rage.

"How would you like it if someone shoved a metal bar in your mouth and then jumped on you? She's never been ridden before, the least you could do is make it as painless as possible!" Rosie said loudly, glaring up at the cowboy. Bill didn't know what to say. He was amazed that the mare had stopped fighting the moment she'd seen the girl.

Dancer sighed shakily as Rosie's hand touched her muzzle softly. The girl looked around at the small crowd of people that had gathered.

"She's a wild horse, and she has every right to be frightened. If you were her, wouldn't you fight back too?" asked the girl simply. The crowd began murmuring. Rosie hugged Dancer's nose tightly before continuing.

"You see? I have been visiting her every night, and she trusts me. All it took was a little kindness. I bet I could even ride her without a problem," she said confidently, looking at Dancer with a question in her eye. The mare bobbed her head slightly, and Rosie grinned broadly.

Bill dismounted and shook his head. "Not a chance, missy. This mare is wild and could easily hurt you pretty badly. And besides, you've not ridden as many mustangs as I have. You don't know how they react to things."

Rosie strode up to the saddle and put her foot in the stirrup, promptly mounting the mare. Bill tried to move forward and pull her down, but Dancer shoved him back with her nose, glaring at him angrily. He didn't try again.

Dancer proceeded to walk calmly around the corral without Rosie so much as touching the reins. A hush fell over the crowd as they witnessed what they considered a miraculous happening.

Rosie's parents stood nearest to the rail, her father wrapping a supportive arm around her mother, who was watching in horror.

"Rose Elizabeth Learson! Get down off of that animal this very instant!" Rosie's mother called furiously. Rosie smiled and waved at her parents jovially, and then patted Dancer's neck.

"She won't hurt me, Mama. Lady is my friend. We've spent a lot of time together over the past few days. She wants to let me ride her," Rosie replied quietly.

After one more round of the corral, Rosie jumped off of the mare and unbuckled the saddle and bridle, slinging the items over the fence rails. She ducked under the rail and left the corral amidst cheers from the onlookers. Dancer was left alone in the corral, watching the girl leave. She smiled to herself. Rosie was right. They were friends.

6. Back to the Trail

The wagon train left the fort to keep going farther west. Dancer and Titan were tied to the back of Rosie's wagon this time, and plodded along quietly behind it. Rosie sat just inside the wagon box, and would hold out carrots from time to time for the horses.

Titan began to enjoy the girl's company as much as Dancer, and would even allow her to ride along behind the wagon on his broad back.

It was afternoon when the wagons made camp within the borders of the forest. The air had grown rapidly colder, and Dancer felt the sudden change in the wind. It was soon to be winter; the last warm days had come to an end.

51

The cowboys had noticed this change too, and began bundling up the wagon party with blankets and checking on the food supplies. Rosie didn't seem to mind the cold; she kept riding along on Titan's back happily.

It was mid afternoon when the first light snowflakes began to fall. Dancer reached out a long pink tongue and caught one. Rosie giggled softly and reached out her own tongue. Two snowflakes came to rest on it, and she looked at Dancer with a broad grin.

"That's fun!" she said. Dancer snorted and tossed her mane in agreement. Titan looked over at his mate and shook his head in amusement.

"You are definitely a strange mare," he commented teasingly. Dancer laughed.

"Why thank you, you aren't so bad yourself," she replied with a mock air of haughtiness. Titan chuckled.

As the day wore on, the snow began falling more and more heavily. The cowboys began to get more anxious to reach a place of shelter, and hurried the wagons along at a faster than normal pace. Dancer and Titan began to jog to keep from being dragged by their ropes. Rosie had gone back to riding inside the wagon now that the cold was beginning to get worse.

She sat in plain view of the horses, wrapped in three heavy robes to keep out the cold temperature. Dancer and Titan doggedly followed the wagon, trying to fight off the cold themselves.

Rosie held out a carrot to Dancer, who took it carefully from the girl's hand, and then bent her head back down to keep it out of the wind.

The wind howled and whistled as the snow got heavier and heavier. Dancer and Titan kept on, trying to keep from falling in the deep snow. The wagons began to go slower and slower as the mules fought their way through the drifts. The snowfall had now become a raging blizzard, and the two horses could see nothing except the swirling white. They knew that they were still with the wagon train because of the tugging of their lead ropes.

Suddenly, the wagons stopped. The snow had become so deep that the mules could not get through it. They were exhausted, and could go no further. One of the cowboys rode back along the line of wagons and shouted out the information to the bewildered pioneers.

Rosie peered out at Dancer and Titan from her cocoon of robes. She had to strain her eyes to see them in the swirling snow. She made out two dark shapes behind the wagon, and she smiled in relief. All that the wagons could do now was wait for the storm to run its course.

***

A sharp cry was heard over the roaring of the storm. Dancer had dozed off, but the shout startled her. She lifted her head and tried to see through the blizzard, but could see nothing. Titan nudged her worriedly, for he had heard the voice too.

Rosie's face appeared in the back of the wagon. "Mama says that someone is sick. We don't know what to do, there's nobody out here that can help!" she shouted to the horses.

Dancer strained her ears and heard the conversation going on between Rosie's father and the cowboy who was relaying the news.

"I don't know what to do, sir. If we don't get help, the little lass will die. The only thing I can think of is if someone were to go back to the fort for help. But it's suicide to try something as foolish as that."

Rosie's father agreed. "Don't let anyone leave the wagon train. We've got talented women amongst us. Surely they can help the girl until the snow stops. We have no other choice."

The cowboy left then, and the conversation ended. Dancer heard Rosie crying in the wagon, and moved forward, sticking her head into the wagon box. The girl was still wrapped in her heavy robes; tears streaming down her face. She saw Dancer, and the tears began afresh as she stammered out what was happening.

"It's Betsey, my friend. She's got a terrible fever from the cold, and they say she probably won't last the week. Oh Lady, I wish there was something I could do!" she exclaimed desperately. Dancer nuzzled the girl's hair softly.

Suddenly, a determined light filled Rosie's eyes, and she looked up at the mare eagerly.

"I know what I can do! The cowboy said that we needed someone to go back to the fort to get help! If I ride you, we could get there and back by the time the blizzard ends!" she said.

Dancer stared at her young friend in shock. It was a very dangerous idea. The storms lulled for no one, not even a sick child. There was very little chance that they would even find the fort, much less make it there alive. The mare shook her head stubbornly, refusing to put Rosie in danger like that. But the girl simply placed her hands on her hips and stared at the horse.

"We have to do this, Lady. For Betsey."

The words were so simply spoken, so innocent, that Dancer felt her heart ache at Rosie's fear for her friend. But still…

Rosie didn't give her time to think. The girl wrapped her robes tighter and made her way over the back of the wagon and down onto the wooden ledge in front of Dancer. She gripped the mare's mane tightly for support, and managed to swing a leg over the horse's dark gray back. Dancer couldn't move aside for fear of dropping her young friend. She turned her head over her shoulder and gave Rosie a look that plainly said: *there is no way I am going anywhere.*

The girl leaned forward and untied Dancer's rope from the wagon box. Pulling Dancer's head around, she looked into the mare's dark eyes.

"If you help me now, I promise that I will free you and your mate when we return," she said. Dancer's eyes lit for a moment, and then the excitement left them again, and she tossed her head. As much as she wanted her freedom, she wasn't willing to put Rosie in path of danger.

Rosie's eyes filled with tears. "Please girl, we can't let Betsey die," she said in a soft whisper. Over the howling of the wind, Dancer barely caught the words. But she heard them. And she made her decision. She looked quickly over at Titan, who was asleep, his head hung down to protect it from the snow.

The mare softly lipped his black mane, and then turned and vanished into the blizzard, Rosie holding onto the lead rope.

***

Titan raised his head slightly and looked to his left. It took him a moment to realize that Dancer was gone. He stared at the empty space beside him, and realized that her rope had not broken…it had been untied. He peered with snow-crusted eyes into the back of the wagon, and saw only Rosie's mother sleeping amidst the heavy

56

blankets. The stallion reared up, bellowing with all his might. The woman inside the wagon started up, and saw the big black horse rearing.

She screamed in fright, but stopped when Titan's bellowing ceased. He stood in the snow, tossing his head. The woman looked down at the blankets where her daughter had been sleeping, and her eyes widened with shock when she realized that Rosie was not there.

"Robert!" the woman screamed up to her sleeping husband. The man woke instantly, and looked down at her in confusion.

"What's wrong, Hannah?" he shouted back. Rosie's mother pointed frantically to the empty blankets.

"Rosie's gone, Robert! And the mare is gone too! What are we going to do! She's probably lost out in the storm! Robert! We've got to do something!" she screamed in a panic. The man crawled down into the wagon, and put his arms around his wife.

"Hannah, I don't want to worry you, but I think Rosie might've tried to go for help for Betsey. She overheard my conversation with Tex. We'd best pray with everything we've got. But there is a good thing in all of this. She's with the mare, and the horse has good sense; she'll take care of our girl. Plus, the mare's carrying a young'n, so they won't get very far."

Titan, who had been listening to the conversation with grave interest, suddenly found himself staring at the couple in the wagon. Dancer, pregnant? The very thought of it stunned him into total silence. Were they really going to be parents?

The big black stood wearily amidst the swirling snow, his mind darting here and there as he thought about what it all meant. His thoughts were broken by the soft sobs of Rosie's mother from inside the wagon.

***

Dancer was lost. She could see nothing but the raging blizzard, the swirling white, everywhere she looked. Her eyes and nose were frosted and coated with a thin layer of ice. Rosie still clung to the mare's mane, but Dancer could not tell if her passenger was awake or not.

A dread feeling of helplessness overwhelmed Dancer. She knew that she should never have agreed to this madness. A question rose in her mind: Were they going to die?

Relentlessly Dancer trudged on through the drifts of snow, sinking in nearly to her chest. Her legs began to feel weaker and weaker as she exerted more and more strength to try and get them through the blizzard.

Hours passed, and Dancer's steady pace was reduced to a staggering plod. She doggedly kept on, refusing to let Rosie die.

Suddenly, her head hit something hard and rough. She peered through the layer of ice that covered her eyes, and saw the trunk of a tree. Moving slightly beyond the tree, she quickly realized that she had entered a copse of tall trees, whose branches created a natural canopy over a small clear area. Only a few inches of snow covered the ground beneath the trees.

It was a natural shelter from the raging storm, and Dancer felt relief sweep through her. She fell to her knees in exhaustion, and felt Rosie slide off of her back. The girl landed in the soft snow, and her eyes fluttered open weakly. She glanced around, and then her gaze fell on the horse in front of her.

"You did it, girl. You got us to a safe place," she whispered. Dancer nuzzled Rosie's face gently, and Rosie stiffly put her arms around the mare's head, hugging it to her. Dancer suddenly felt a deep sense of loyalty building within her. She knew then that she would gladly give her life for Rosie's safety. She knew now how her father had felt toward Running Fox, the Indian chieftain.

Rosie leaned back and looked into the mare's eyes. "I love you, girl," she said quietly. Dancer sighed contentedly, and closed her eyes.

Together, girl and horse fell asleep amidst the raging storm, oblivious to its existence.

7. The Storm Breaks

Dancer opened her eyes slowly. The wind had stopped its dreadful howling. She rose to her feet, taking care not to disturb Rosie, who was still sleeping.

The mare peered out from their small haven, and saw that the blizzard had ended. The snow was deep, but had ceased to fall. Dancer looked around quickly for anything that she could recognize. There was nothing, except...

Dancer suddenly felt her heart leap for joy. A dark brown dot in the distance she had seen, but had known nonetheless that it was the fort that they had left merely two days ago. She began to prance about in excitement, whinnying happily. They had made it after all!

The horse's frenzied movements woke the sleeping girl, who sat up slowly to see what all the fuss was about. Seeing Dancer's antics, Rosie stood up, wavering slightly from exhaustion. The mare moved to the girl's side, and Rosie grabbed onto Dancer's mane for support.

"Thanks, girl," Rosie said softly, and with a little help from Dancer, made her way up onto the mare's broad gray back. Dancer trotted out into the deep snow, her hooves making crunching sounds as she trudged along. Rosie suddenly spotted the fort, and she knew why Dancer had been so excited.

"We did it, girl! We made it!" Rosie shouted euphorically. She gripped Dancer's mane extra tight, and the mare understood the cue. She flattened her ears and lunged forward, charging through the drifts of snow, sheets of white flying up from her hooves.

The fort drew nearer and nearer with every stride Dancer took, until it was only a few hundred yards away. A shout rang from the wall top, and the gates began to slowly open. The gray mare and her rider flashed through them into the fort. Exclamations of surprise emanated from several of the traders as they rushed to help Rosie off of the mare.

Both travelers were exhausted. Rosie was pulled off of Dancer's back and hurried towards a small cabin. The girl struggled feebly.

"My horse! Lady!" she cried out weakly, her small fists clenched. The man who carried her squeezed her hand reassuringly.

"Don't you worry, lil' miss. We'll make sure yer hoss is well cared for," he said quietly, his eyes full of worry for the nearly frozen youngster. Rosie was carried into the cabin, and the man set her down on a pile of furs. A middle-aged woman stoked the fire and tucked warm blankets around Rosie's chin.

The man who had carried Rosie came back outside. He frowned as he saw Dancer standing in the same place she had been when they had left with the girl. All of the effort that it had taken to lunge through the snow had left Dancer completely exhausted.

Reaching a hand up to the tangled gray mane, the man patted the mare quietly. Dancer raised dark eyes to survey him imperiously. The man smiled at her.

"Don'tcha worry, old gal. Pete'll take care of you," he said softly. Dancer snorted, and eyed him again. He put a rope halter carefully around her head and led her toward the corral. Dancer recognized it as the same one that she had occupied the last time she had been inside the fort. But it did not seem like a cage anymore. It was a place of solitude and rest.

Pete threw a bit of hay into the corral, and then retreated back to the cabin. Dancer lipped a bite of hay, and savored it gratefully. She had been feeling a bit nauseous, and the food tasted good. After finishing her meal, she sank to her knees carefully. Stretching out her dark neck, Dancer rolled onto her side, and fell asleep.

***

Dancer ran through the meadow of wildflowers, her hooves pounding the grasses as she skimmed along like a bird in flight. She tossed her mane, pure happiness coursing through her. A dark shape appeared to her right, running alongside her. With a whinny of joy, Dancer recognized Titan. The big stallion looked at her proudly. He faded into the distance, and Dancer slid to a stop, her nostrils flaring. In front of her lay a pure black colt, sleeping in the warmth of the afternoon sun.

Curiously, Dancer stared at the tiny creature in wonder. She reached down with her nose and touched the little colt's fuzzy side. The baby woke, and looked up at her, his eyes bright. He whickered quietly, and stared back at her. Dancer felt a strange feeling rising within her. The colt looked just like Titan!

Dancer backed away from the colt, her mind whirling in confusion. Was she seeing Titan as a baby? And if so, why? She didn't understand. Dancer turned around, but the meadow was gone. In its place was a burning forest. Flames reached up above the treetops, destroying everything in their path.

Fear took Dancer. Fear like she had never known before. She turned to run, but another wall of fire blocked her escape. The flames closed in around her…

"Lady! Lady! " said a voice softly into Dancer's ear. The mare woke up quickly, and her head lifted from the snow. Rosie put her arms around Dancer's head, and hugged her close.

"It's alright, girl! You must've been dreaming something horrible," said the girl. Dancer looked around, startled. There was no fire, no colt...just Rosie. Dancer sighed deeply. It had been a dream. But so real...

Rosie released the mare's head, and sat back. She was wrapped in buffalo robes, and her face still held a pale tinge, but she definitely looked better than she had. Sunlight warmed Dancer, and she lurched to her feet. She steadied her legs, and looked questioningly at Rosie.

"Oh, don't worry, girl. They sent some men out to the wagon train, and a woman as well, who knows a lot about healing people. Betsey will be fine. We have to stay here until its safe to go back."

Dancer tossed her mane, and shook herself. Rosie came up to her and placed a hand on Dancer's side. She smiled up at the mare. Dancer looked back at her, confused. Her eyes questioned Rosie, but the girl just giggled and shook her head. Dancer felt frustrated, and pinned her ears back slightly. What was Rosie hiding from her?

The girl sensed Dancer's uneasiness. "I'm sorry girl. It's just so wonderful! You're going to have a foal! Pete said so!" burst out Rosie excitedly. Dancer's eyes widened.

Shock crept into Dancer's mind. She couldn't believe it. Was it really true? Was that the foal that she had seen in her dream? What was happening to her? It was all so much to take in at once. Her breathing slowed as she drew deeper breaths. Rosie patted Dancer's shoulder, and the two of them stood in silence for a long while before Rosie finally turned around to go back to the cabin.

***

It wasn't long before Pete and several other trappers took Rosie and Dancer back to the wagon train. Once in sight of the familiar wagons, Rosie leaped off of Dancer's back and ran through the snow to her mother's waiting arms.

"Lady kept me safe, Mama. She saved us," said Rosie through her tears. Hannah held her daughter tightly, as if she would never let go, her own tears falling down into Rosie's brown hair. She looked up at Dancer with such a look of gratitude that the mare felt slightly embarrassed.

Then Titan came toward her. Dancer saw the big black approaching, and her eyes lowered slightly. She expected him to be angry. But if Titan was angry, he didn't show it at all. The onlookers gave a gasp at the sight before them.

The two horses stood in the snow, a ray of sunlight illuminating them. Their muzzles touched gently, and Titan pressed his forehead to Dancer's. Rosie stared at the horses in amazement. The sight touched every heart that saw it, even the hardened cowboys.

Dancer's eyes rose to Titan's, and she sighed deeply. "I missed you," she whispered to him. The stallion nodded slightly, and blew into Dancer's face softly.

"I was afraid for you," he said. "I was afraid that you would never return to me. Promise me that you will never, ever do that again." His voice was low and gruff, and Dancer could tell that he was trying to hide how he really felt. Her heart melted under his dark eyes.

"I promise…and Titan, there's something else that I want you to know," she began. She felt suddenly uncomfortable. Titan smiled.

"I already know," he said. At Dancer's confused look, he continued. "I heard Rosie's father mention it when they found out that you had gone. We are going to be parents," he said softly. Dancer nodded contentedly, and leaned against her mate's shoulder. Things were going to be just fine.

***

Rosie kept her promise. That very night, she lowered herself down onto the wooden ledge at the back of her wagon, and untied the horses' ropes from the wood. Tears glistened in her eyes as she stroked Dancer's neck for the last time. The mare felt torn between leaving and staying, but Rosie's next words put her doubts to rest.

67

"Don't you worry about me, girl. I want you to be free. I want your baby to be free too. Go back to being the wild horses that you used to be. But…promise you'll never forget me," she said, choking back sobs. Dancer pressed her head to Rosie's, her long forelock falling over the girl's face. Rosie smiled, and slipped the halters from the horses' faces.

"Good. Now go, and be free," the girl whispered, her hand gently pushing Dancer away. Both horses whirled and galloped through the snow and into the forest. Rosie held Dancer's rope halter close, and crawled back inside the wagon.

***

Dancer and Titan did not stop running for a long time. The snow was light and fluffy and the two horses did not have any trouble getting through it.

The first pinkish hues of the sunrise had just begun to stretch out over the sky as the two weary travelers took a short rest from their relentless pace. Both of them had resolved to get back to Dancer's herd. They would stop to visit Titan's family on the way back, and see if Lily had made it home.

Dancer wanted to see her parents more than anything else. She missed them terribly, and was eager to share her exciting news with them. From what she and Titan could figure out, they had about eight months left to wait before their foal was born. Dancer was excited. She had told Titan about her dream, and frequently wondered if the baby was going to be a little black colt, just like the one she had seen.

The two of them bedded down quietly, neither one having the energy for conversation. They had traveled a long ways, and were both ready to rest themselves.

***

The familiar forest came within sight soon after the two horses began their journey once again in the morning. Titan whinnied happily. They were almost home! They broke into a canter, and fought the urge to race towards the trees. Titan slowed his pace slightly, trying to keep Dancer from exerting herself too much.

"Slow down, my love. I don't want you to hurt the..." his voice faded as Dancer stared at him.

"Titan, I know you're just being concerned, but I am fine. A little bit of cantering is not going to kill me. I promise," she said with a smile. Titan said no more, but Dancer saw him bite his lip to keep from speaking.

The two horses lunged into the trees, and crashed through the underbrush, moving closer to the valley with every stride. The forest flashed by them as they raced toward the familiar territory.

Emerging from the trees, the two horses stopped at the top of the ridge overlooking the valley. Down below them, a very familiar group of horses were grazing peacefully in the morning sun. Titan reared up and bellowed loudly. The gray stallion at the far end of the herd threw up his head and returned the greeting instantly, and bedlam broke out among the horses.

Dancer and Titan lunged down towards them, their hooves creating mini rockslides down the steep valley wall as they slowly made their way towards the herd.

The reunion was joyful. Fleetstar welcomed them heartily, as did the rest of the herd. Questions came from all sides as the horses begged for the story of Dancer and Titan's journey. Fleetstar finally silenced them all by emitting a sharp whistle.

"Enough! Let them breathe; they have traveled very far, and are weary. There will be time for stories later. Right now, however, I am sure that you are both wondering about a certain filly…" he said, his voice fading. The sound of quiet hoof beats sounded from behind the herd.

Lily came galloping up to them, her eyes brimming with tears. "Dancer! Titan! You are both home!" she exclaimed, her whole expression the image of joy. Dancer laughed aloud.

"Lily, we worried about you so much! Titan never gave up hope that you had found your way home."

Titan stepped forward and nudged his sister affectionately. "I am glad to see you, little sister. How did you find your way home? What happened after you escaped from the humans?" he asked curiously. Lily tossed her mane.

"I was lost for a while, but I eventually found some landmarks that were familiar, and was able to make it back. Father was so afraid for you both. He told me that he would never be able to face your parents, Dancer, if you never returned."

Dancer smiled at the older stallion, who looked completely content now that his son and his friend's daughter had returned. Titan broke the silence.

"Father, I have two pieces of news that will make you very happy," he said with a mysterious glint in his eyes. Fleetstar cocked his head sideways and looked expectantly at his son. Titan looked at Dancer, who nodded.

Turning back to the herd, Titan announced, "Dancer and I have become mates, and we are expecting a foal this fall!"

The thunder of the herd's exultation deafened them.

8. A Life Worth Living

Dancer's sides rose and fell as she breathed. Titan
stood vigilantly over his mate as she slept. The night sky
twinkled with tiny stars, and a cool autumn breeze wafted
through the valley.

Lily softly stepped up to her brother, and looked
down at her sleeping sister-in-law. "Is she alright?" she
asked quietly. Titan glanced at his sister and nodded. The
two of them watched the black mare worriedly. She had
been very listless lately, and had not been eating well.
Both knew that Dancer's time was drawing very near, and
that they could be blessed with the sight of the foal any
day.

Dancer and Titan had decided to stay with Titan's
father's herd until the foal was born, so that Fleetstar and
the herd would be able to see the new foal when it
arrived.

The prospect of being a father made Titan slightly apprehensive. He had no idea how to raise this foal to be worthy of the bloodlines it carried. He sighed deeply. He was tired of waiting, but he knew that no matter how much he wanted the foal to be born for all their sakes, it would come when it was good and ready, and not a second before.

Secretly, Titan hoped for a colt, but he knew that Dancer wanted a filly, so he kept his hope to himself.

Dancer stirred slightly, her dark eyes opening to look up at her mate and his sister. She raised her head and shook her mane wearily. Her legs were thrust out in front of her, and she slowly staggered up, the extra weight of the foal making that small movement difficult.

"Is something wrong?" she asked the two horses standing next to her, concern lining her face at their stony expressions. Titan shook his head reassuringly.

"No, nothing's wrong. We were just..." he stopped as Dancer's side twitched strangely. Lily gasped. Dancer stared at them, her expression changing from concern to sudden discomfort.

"Titan..." she whispered. The black stallion suddenly began to panic. He raced past his mate towards the herd, waking everyone up with his frantic shouts.

"Everyone wake up! Hurry, you've got to help, Dancer's having the foal! She needs help now! Father, wake everyone up, we've got to hurry! I'm going to be a father!" he announced at the top of his lungs. It was very effective. The entire herd was up, though somewhat groggily, and a couple of older mares slowly made their way towards Dancer. Titan flattened his ears.

"Why are you going so slowly? Don't you care if she is alright?" he demanded angrily. Fleetstar stepped in front of his son sternly, and refused to budge, keeping the frantic stallion away from Dancer.

"Titan, relax! It could be hours before the foal is born. Never rush pregnant mares; it is a very dangerous idea. If you truly want to help Dancer, the best thing you can do is stay as far away from her as possible. She has enough to think about right now without you getting her agitated with your panicking. Mares have been giving us foals for thousands of years. She doesn't need your help."

The older stallion's calm words seemed to soothe Titan. The black stallion sighed, though his breathing was still short and heavy. He nodded, agreeing with his sire. He turned and vanished into the forest. Fleetstar smiled to himself, remembering his own reaction when his mate had given birth to Titan. He had been just as frantic as his son was now. The older stallion shook his head in amusement, and went back to the small group of horses that were gathered around Dancer.

***

The horses around Dancer stepped back to give her room. She trembled slightly before falling heavily to her side. Dancer gritted her teeth, silently bearing her suffering. An old mare called Nona leaned down and spoke to the young gray mare.

"Don't you worry, lassie. You're young an' strong, and the foal is havin' no problems at all. You'll be done before y'know it!" she said encouragingly. Dancer looked up at her gratefully.

"Thank you," she said quietly. The moments that followed felt like lifetimes to the horses that were waiting eagerly to see the foal of their chieftain's son. Lily could hardly contain her excitement. She was going to be an aunt! And with parents like Dancer and Titan, the foal was sure to be beautiful.

A hush fell over the group, and the only sound to be heard was Dancer's deep breathing. The young mare closed her eyes, and knew that if Titan were with her, he would be bursting with pride. He was so excited to be a father, and she knew that he would be a good one.

Her thoughts were interrupted by the sudden recession of the pain, gasps of the herd members, and Nona's deep voice making the long awaited announcement.

"It's a colt! Titan has a son!"

Dancer craned her neck over her shoulder, and saw a pure black bundle lying in the grass behind her. Its tiny head shook as it struggled to free itself from the constricting sac.

A motherly whicker sounded from the weary mare's throat. As tired as she was, she knew that she had to tell her son that she was here, and that she loved him. A shrill squeak responded, and the herd chuckled softly. Lily moved forward and nudged the foal around so that he was facing his mother.

The tiny colt's damp ears perked up, and his eyes brightened. Through his still blurry vision, he could see the large dark form that was his dam. She nickered again, and he squeaked back. Dancer felt like flying. She was looking at her son. Her son!

Wearily, she lurched to her feet, and raised her muzzle to the sky. A trumpeting neigh erupted from her throat, and the sound echoed around the valley, creating an orchestral boom.

The herd was silent, listening to the exultant announcement of joy from the young mother. Finished with telling the world of her son's arrival, Dancer turned back to the foal. He was watching her quizzically. She smiled at him, a rush of motherly pride filling her heart.

She extended her nose down to him, and he nuzzled her softly, his baby whiskers tickling her muzzle. She tossed her head, and snorted. The colt whinnied, trying out the lustiness of his lungs. The herd members realized the importance of the moment, and retreated, leaving the pair alone to bond.

***

Titan was pacing in circles around the trees, when he heard his mate's trumpet. Thinking something was wrong; he could stand it no longer. He charged from the forest, making for the herd at full speed.

His hooves pounded the ground, flinging up clods of dirt behind him. He lunged into the valley, and abruptly slid to a stop. There in front of him, Dancer was standing, her coat flecked with lather, her gray muzzle extended down to that of an ebony black foal.

The black stallion was hypnotized. He could not keep his eyes from his new son. The tiny colt was a perfect image of his father. He had Dancer's dark, deep eyes, but other than that, he was his father's perfect likeness. The only difference was the white blaze that ran down the colt's little muzzle.

Titan felt as though he were floating on air. Was this possible? He had waited for this moment for so long, that he didn't know what to do. He cantered forward, and Dancer looked up. She saw her mate coming toward her, and her ears pricked forward in welcome.

The meeting of father and son was a moment of magic for Dancer. She saw her mate gently touch his nose to his little son's, and the three of them were bonded together inseparably. They were a family now, and nothing would ever change that.

Titan looked at his mate. "His name is Shalimar," he said softly. Dancer nodded. She liked the name. Shalimar...it was the name worthy of the descendant of Sariavo.

***

The little colt grew quickly. It wasn't two days before he was trying to run around after his parents. Shalimar was continually learning new words, and was now putting sentences together. He was a source of joy for the whole herd, most especially Fleetstar, who was completely taken with his little grandson. He began to teach Shalimar about life as a wild mustang, and the laws of survival.

Titan was taking his fatherly responsibilities very seriously. Dancer saw him take Shalimar into the forest every day, the two of them having a philosophical discussion about trees and forests.

As for Dancer, she was content to nurse her son and to give him all the love she could. Her pride for her little colt was very strong, but even stronger was her sense of protection. Her eyes constantly stayed on her son, unless he was safe with his father or grandfather. She would never risk the chance of him wandering off.

Though Dancer was content staying with Titan's herd, she frequently wished that she could go back to her own herd. She missed her parents a lot, and wanted them to have an equal part in the raising of Shalimar. Though Fleetstar was a very good grandsire, Dancer knew that her own father would teach her son the ways of a Mighty

Stallion. And that was more important than anything else. Her son should be taught to follow in the footsteps of his ancestors.

She voiced her wish to Titan one night as they were lying in the grass, Shalimar sleeping soundly between them. The stallion was not very surprised, since he knew that she would want to return to her home sooner or later. It was completely understandable.

"I understand. I will tell my father in the morning, and we will leave tomorrow afternoon. Is that alright with you?" he asked. Dancer nodded, her eyes downcast. She finally spoke again.

"Titan, I'm sorry that I am asking you to leave your family. If you don't want to go, I will respect that. This is your home, and your herd. It would be alright if you decide not to leave. I would not..."

Titan interrupted her. "Dancer..." he paused;, waiting for her to look at him. When she finally did, he continued.

"I want you to be able to see your family again. It has been a year and a half since you last saw them, and it would not be fair of me to restrain you when you are so close to them. So do not worry yourself over it. We will leave tomorrow, and we will bring Shalimar to the home of his ancestors."

Dancer smiled gratefully. "Thank you, Titan. I love you so much," she whispered softly. Titan stretched out his nose to her, and their muzzles touched gently. The two of them stretched out in the grass to sleep, needing rest for their journey in the morning.

***

Fleetstar was very sad when his son told him their plan to leave, but the old stallion had known that the day would eventually come. He looked over toward his daughter-in-law and grandson, and sighed.

"I will not say that this news does not grieve me, but I know that she must miss her parents. Go now, with my blessing. Just promise that you will return someday," he asked. Titan nodded instantly.

"Of course, Father. We will visit as often as we can. Shalimar will never forget his grandsire. We will take very good care of him, and someday he will be as famous as Sariavo."

Fleetstar chuckled at this. "Indeed! Of that, I have no doubts. And I will pray every night for his continued safety."

There were no goodbyes said. Titan turned and trotted back to his mate and son, leaving Fleetstar watching him go. The old stallion kept his eyes on his son's family until the three figures were lost to sight in the forest trees.

"God keep you safe," he whispered into the breeze.

***

Shalimar's excitement was contagious. He was very eager to go on an "adventure" with his parents, and was equally impatient to meet his other grandparents. Dancer kept him fascinated with stories of his grandfather and great-grandfathers as they traveled along.

Titan kept silent, his eyes never ceasing their roving as he watched their surroundings. He knew that this part of the forest was home to many predators who would not hesitate to try and attack the young colt - especially the mountain lions that roamed the forests. They were always trying to find an easy meal.

The little colt ran a little ways ahead and gave a little joyful buck. Dancer instantly caught up with him and shook her head sternly.

"Don't get separated from us, Shalimar. This is a very dangerous forest, and I don't want you to get lost. There are very bad animals in these woods. Do you understand?"

The little colt nodded vigorously. "Yes, Mama. I unnerstand. How farther izzit to Gramma and Granda's?" he asked, his baby language still slightly hard to understand. Dancer nuzzled her son lovingly.

"You little impatient one. Don't worry, its not much farther. We'll be there before night comes."

***

Dancer was the first to top the hill in front of the cave. She looked down over the clearing, and her eyes traveled over the waterfall and the stream, the mossy rocks, and finally, the opening of the cave itself. A wonderful sensation filled her. She was home at last!

She slowly went down the hill, and trotted up to the pool. The water swirled gently, as clear as ever. The shallows were inviting and seemed to welcome Dancer home. She extended her neck and took a long drink from the cool water. It was immediately refreshing. Titan joined her, but Shalimar was too excited. He pranced around his parents.

"Where is ever'body?" he asked curiously. Dancer was beginning to wonder that herself. But her questions were soon put to rest.

A familiar white stallion came up to the cave's mouth. He stared at the three travelers, and his mouth opened slightly, but no words were spoken. His surprise was evident. A buckskin mare joined him, and was not so hesitant to welcome them. She raced out to her daughter, and Dancer laughed aloud.

"Mother! I am home...home to stay!" she exclaimed. Glory came up then, his dark eyes brimming with tears of joy as he looked at how much his daughter had changed. It had been nearly two years, and she had now become a fine young mare. And...

It was then that Glory and Secret noticed Shalimar. The two older horses stared at him in shock, for there was no doubt as to who this colt had come from. He was the very image of his parents, and Glory knew right away that this was his grandson. He looked up at Dancer, the pride in his eyes overwhelming.

"This…this is your son," he said. It was not a question, but a simple confirmation of what he already knew. Dancer nodded anyways, and felt tears well up in her own eyes. Glory returned his gaze to Shalimar, who was watching him curiously.

"And what is your name?" the old gray stallion asked of his grandson. Shalimar suddenly became shy.

"Sha'mar…" he whispered. Glory looked up at Dancer questioningly, and she shook her head with a smile.

"His name is Shalimar, Father." Her tone was warm and loving as she spoke the name of her son. Glory looked down at the colt, who nodded vehemently. The old stallion smiled.

"The name of the next Mighty Stallion. Truly, he will be a great name that will be spoken in reverence in the years to come."

***

Dancer left the cave that night, stepping out into the cool night air. The sound of the waterfall made her feel glad to be back. Glory was completely devoted to his grandson, and had promised Dancer to teach the colt all he knew about being a true Mighty Stallion.

Her grandsire Fury had also been very impressed by the young one's size and intelligence. The old stallion was getting on in years, but he too, wanted to take part in the colt's upbringing.

The gray mare was nothing but a shadow in the darkness as she moved into the trees. The wind began to strengthen, whipping back her mane. Dancer raised her nose to the sky and took a long, deep breath of the fresh, wild smelling air. She sighed contentedly. This was where she belonged.

She had not told Titan yet, but Shalimar was not to be their only foal. She was pregnant again, and in her heart, she knew that it would be a colt.

Dancer looked up through the leafy tree branches at the twinkling stars. She knew that this was the place where her sons would grow up, in the birthplace of their ancestors, and the home of Sariavo. It was as it should be. The two colts would grow up to be powerful stallions, running as free as the wind through the pines.

THE END

Epilogue

Dancer did have another son. This time, the colt was a brilliant dapple gray. The proud parents named him Storm for his color, and also because of his more temperamental nature.

Shalimar loved his little brother from the start, and took it upon himself to "teach" Storm about being a stallion. Their story doesn't end here. It will continue very soon...

A Note to My Readers...

A few of you may have noticed that in the <u>Mighty Stallion 3 Glory's Legend</u> "Sneak Peak" section, the plot description for Mighty Stallion 4 was different than the actual book you have just read.

After rereading my initial draft of Mighty Stallion 4, I decided to change Dancer's story and take it in a new direction. That is one of the joys of writing fiction. Remember when you write your own fictional stories, that you can always change things as you go if you find a better idea along the way.

Don't Miss These Other Exciting Stories form the Mighty Stallion Series!

Mighty Stallion

Join Fury's father, Sariavo, the mighty stallion, as he embarks on the grand adventure that started it all.

Mighty Stallion 2 Fury's Journey

Sariavo's son, Fury, is determined to carry on his stepfather's line as a Mighty Stallion. Accompanied by his beautiful mate, Novana, Fury strikes out on his own to prove his adulthood and discovers his destiny.

Mighty Stallion 3 Glory's Legend

This is the exciting story of Fury's son Glory. Travel with him to an Indian tribe, where he befriends the chief, and discovers the meaning of true friendship

About The Author...

Victoria Kasten was born in 1991. She has loved horses since she could walk. She began taking English riding lessons at age nine, and continued with the lessons until age thirteen.

She has two horses, a mischievous Quarter Horse/Pony of America gelding named Looky, and a beautiful registered bay Quarter Horse mare named Katie.

She discovered her love of writing at age eight, when she wrote a short story called The Wild Mustang. She also began to write poems, two of which were published in a national Christian newspaper.

Her first Mighty Stallion book was begun in 2001, at age ten; and finished the year after, at age twelve.

Victoria hopes to be able to be a full time author after she finishes college. She enjoys many hobbies such as researching Medieval History; spending time outside on her family's farm with her cats, rabbits, horses and alpacas; and having squirt gun fights with her parents.